Millie Marotta's

Secrets of the Sea

First published in the United Kingdom in 2021 by
Batsford
43 Great Ormond Street
London
WC1N 3HZ

An imprint of B. T. Batsford Holdings Limited

ISBN 978 1 84994 710 7

A CIP catalogue record for this book is available from the British Library.

30 29 28 27 26 25
20 19 18 17 16 15 14 13 12

Reproduction by Mission Productions, Hong Kong
Printed and bound by Dream Colour, China

This book can be ordered direct from the publisher at
www.batsfordbooks.com, or try your local bookshop

Distributed throughout the UK and Europe by Abrams & Chronicle Books,
1 West Smithfield, London EC1A 9JU and 57 rue Gaston Tessier, 75166 Paris, France

www.abramsandchronicle.co.uk
info@abramsandchronicle.co.uk

Millie Marotta's

Secrets of the Sea

a colouring book adventure

BATSFORD

Introduction

When I think of the sea, the first thing that springs to my mind is the astonishing array of wildlife. Covering close to three-quarters of Earth's surface, oceans create the largest habitat on the planet. From the depths of the seabed to the skies above the waves, they are home to the greatest diversity of life on Earth, from the tiniest microscopic plankton to the gargantuan blue whale. Even in the deepest, darkest ocean trenches, life can be found. As the tides push and pull, and waves swell and crash, shelled creatures scurry across the sea floor, plankton drift at the mercy of the currents, whales and fish roam freely in open waters, and seabirds dip in and out to feed.

When I think of this amazing variety of life, however, the next thing that springs to mind is how threatened it is. I feel the urgency with which we must clean up our seas and safeguard a future for that very wildlife. I live by the sea and walk on the beach or along the coast most days. Nothing blows away the cobwebs like a blast of Welsh sea air! And my dog thinks she's part amphibian, so it's hard to keep her walks restricted to dry land. From one day to the next, these walks are never the same – the weather, light and wildlife differ each time. But what has become an unwelcome constant is the amount of rubbish and debris littering the shoreline. Plastic bags, fishing line, bottles, flip-flops, straws, toys, drink cans and so much more have all found their way onto the beach after drifting on the currents or washed-up during storms. They all pose a huge threat to marine wildlife. And while there is much great work being done to protect and preserve the seas of the world, their health remains increasingly threatened as do the animals that live in and around them.

From the warm bathwater temperatures of the South China sea to the frigid waters off the coast of Antarctica, the colourful show of the Ningaloo reef to the windy, wild waters here at home in Wales, the amazing creatures from different seas around the world have been feeding my curiosity for years. The sea is an environment that is familiar to me and is part of my daily life. So, I'm thrilled to bring you this book of wonderful sea life – a celebration of the sometimes weird but always wonderful species that call our oceans home.

Plunge into a world of swaying kelp forests and dazzling coral reefs, rolling waves and inky deep waters to explore a vibrant world of colour, pattern and texture. From the delicate hues of the blue button jellyfish to the bold geometric pattern of the icon star, the soft pink and greys of seashells to the mesmerizing lightshow of the colour-changing cuttlefish, let your creativity run free as you bring these creatures alive with colour.

You'll find mammals, such as seals and sea otters, who dip in and out of the water. Meet crabs, starfish and snails who crawl and scoot along the seabed. Marvel at dolphins and whales and countless fish who cut through open waters with speed and grace, and enjoy the sea birds who soar and plunge, dip and dive.

Choosing which animals to include in *Secrets of the Sea* was no small feat; I could easily have filled the book three times over. But eventually, I settled on a collection that I hope you will find charming and captivating, from the adorable little auk to the mighty humpback whale, the gentle manatee to gregarious sea lions, and otherworldly sea dragons to the comical Atlantic puffin.

One thing I relish about creating these books is that I get to combine my two passions, art and nature. I have been so heartened by how many of you not only delight in colouring the illustrations themselves but also enjoy learning more of the creatures I have

drawn. For those amongst you who like to know the true colours of the animals or are curious to discover more about them you will find a list of species at the back of the book, where you will also find test pages to try out your colour palettes and materials. And, as ever, there is ample opportunity for you to stretch your creativity further by adding your own drawings and embellishments to your artworks as you go.

Activities that involve using and making things with your hands, such as colouring, have long been regarded as a great way to look after your mental wellbeing. And the same has been said about immersing yourself in nature. So, whether you crack open your colours for a creative burst or a therapeutic escape, with *Secrets of the Sea* I invite you to revel in the brilliance of our natural world. Enjoy a little slice of happy as you unleash your creativity.

Now, without further ado, dive in and explore the world's great oceans. Enrich these secret seas with colour – an ocean adventure awaits.

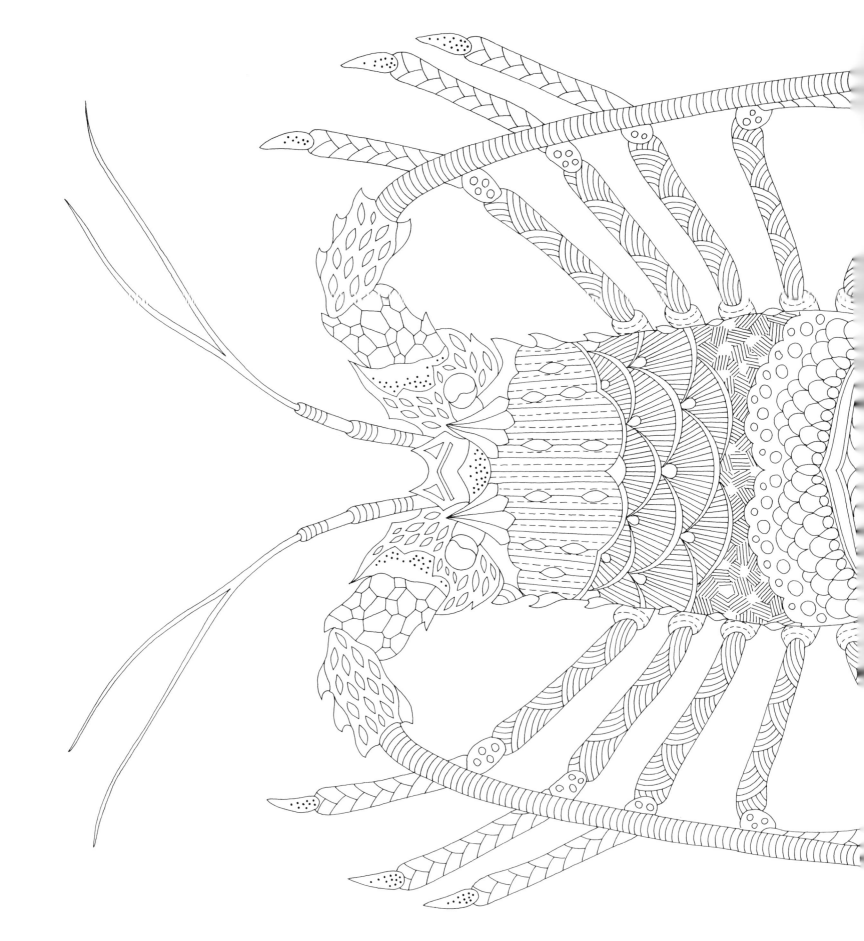

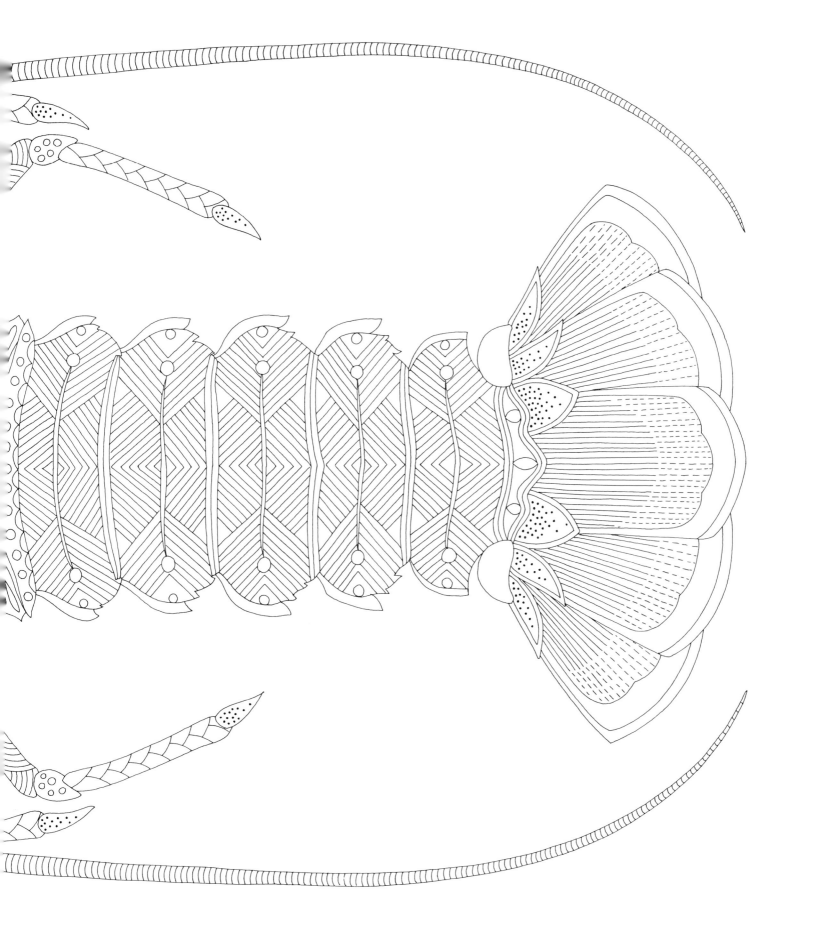

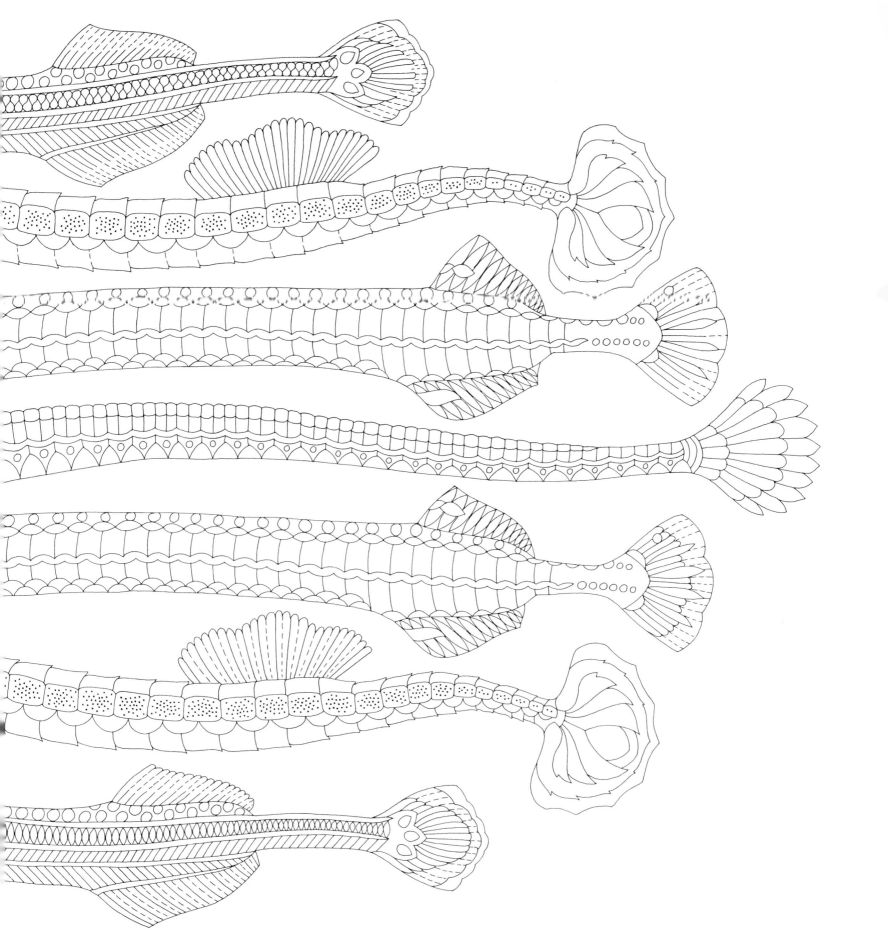

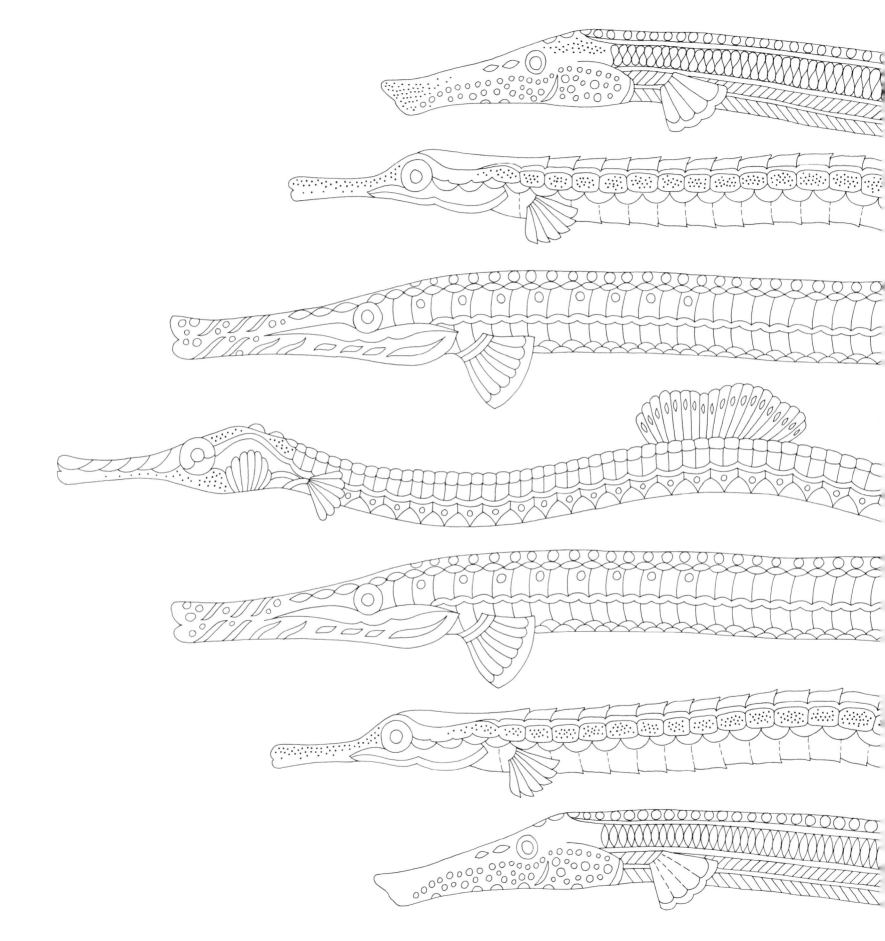

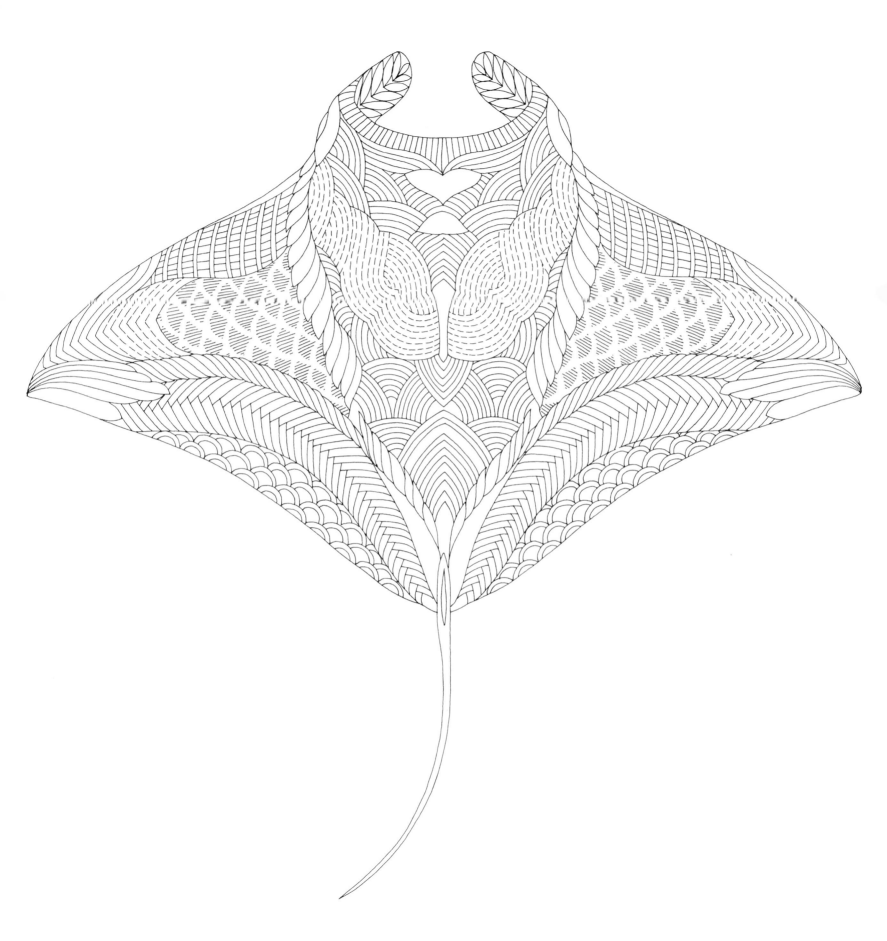

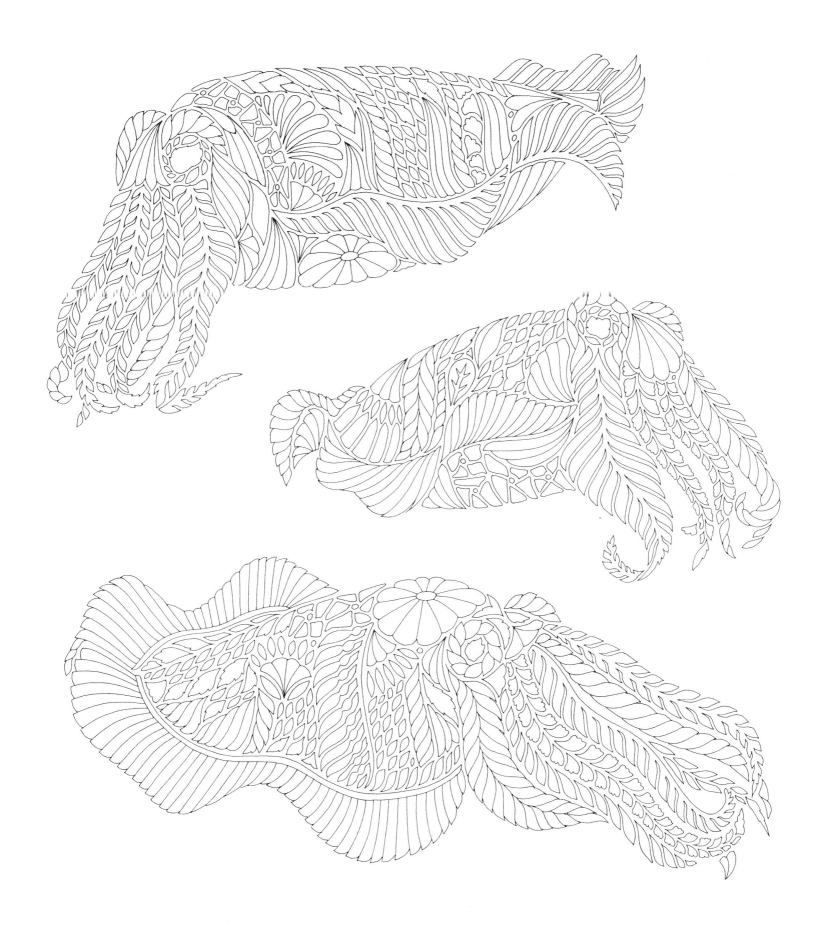

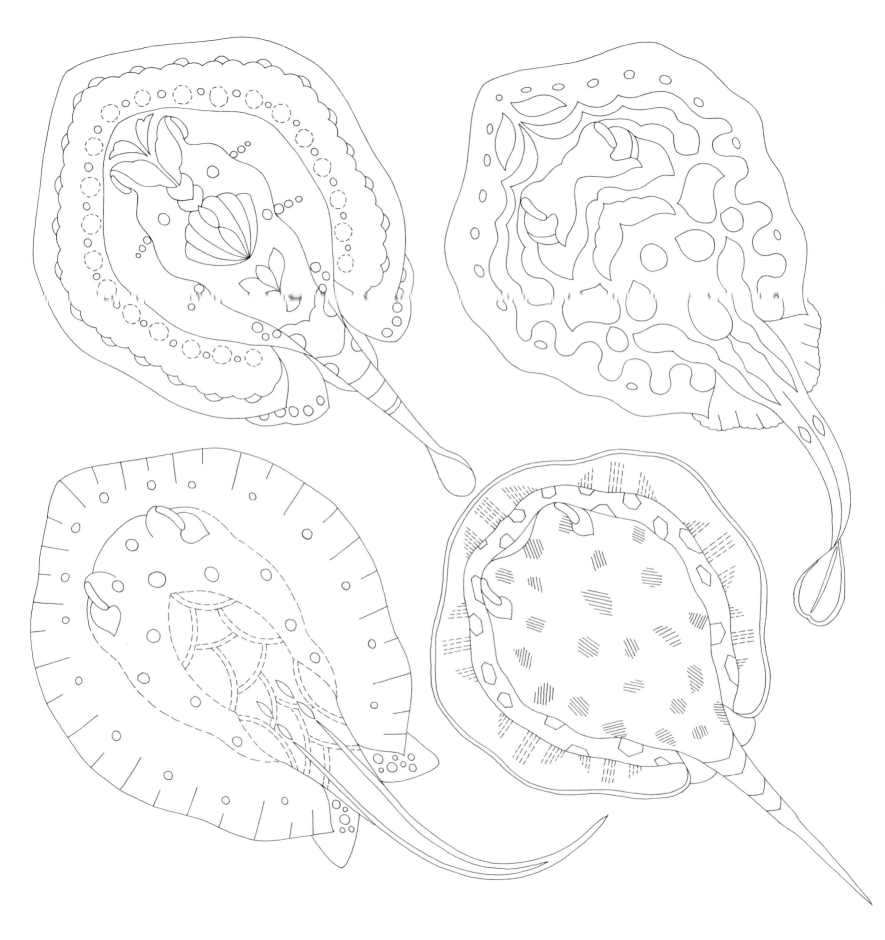

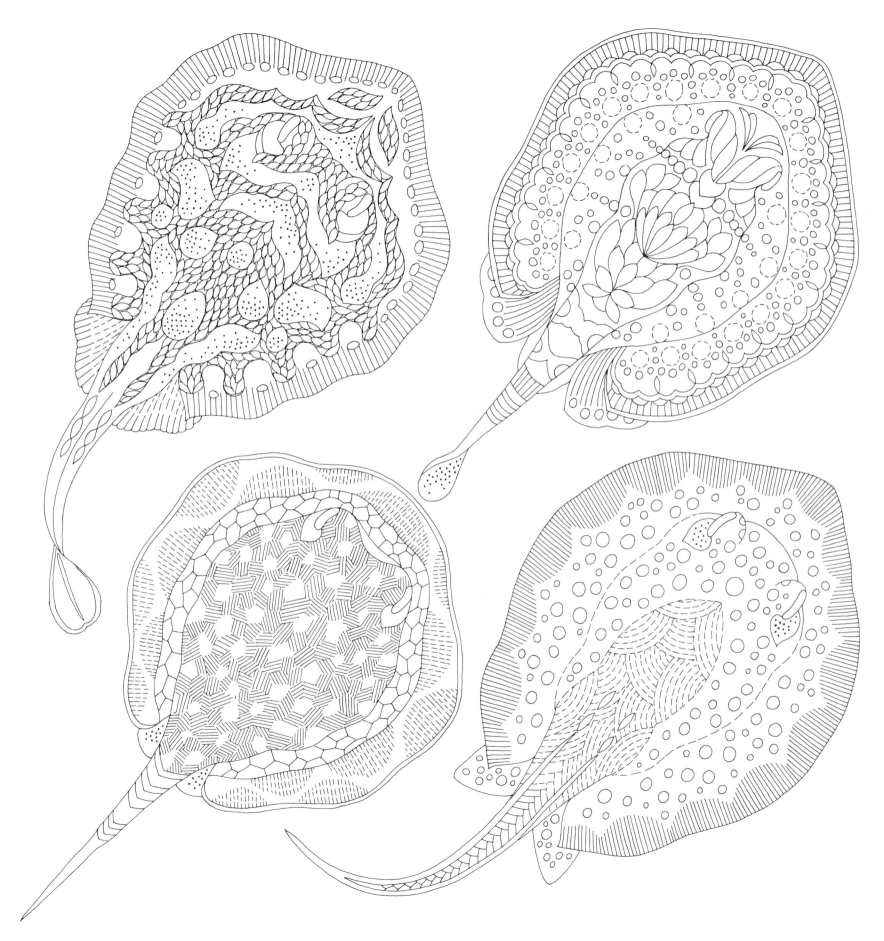

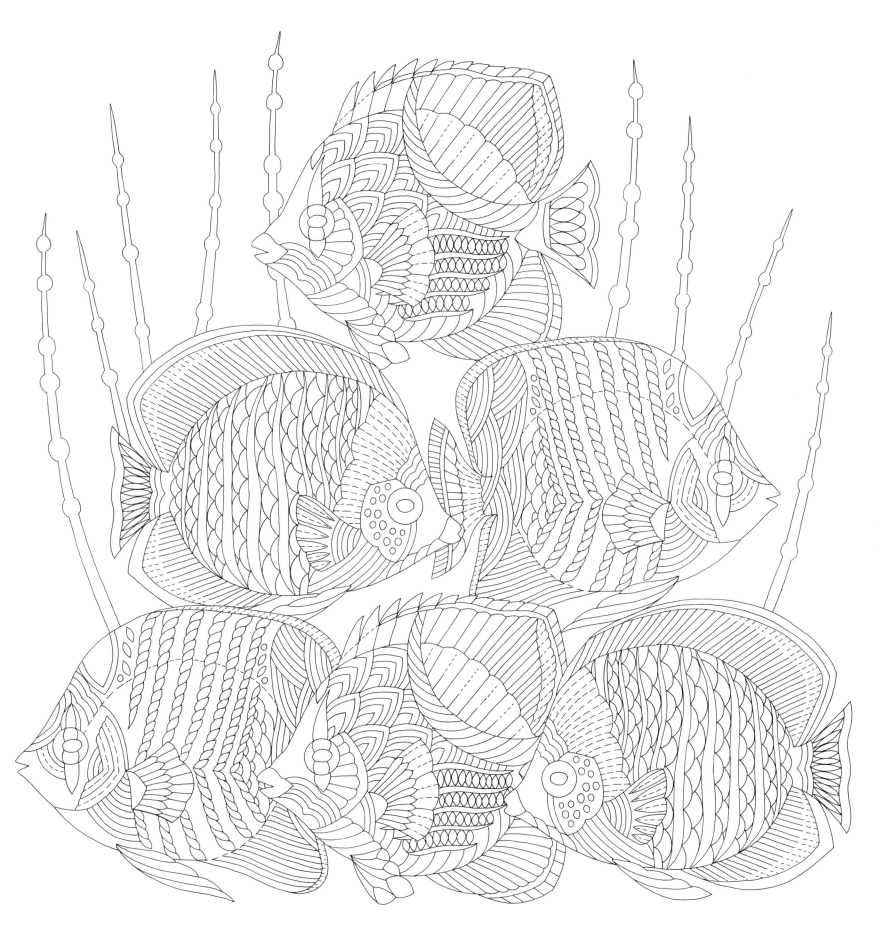

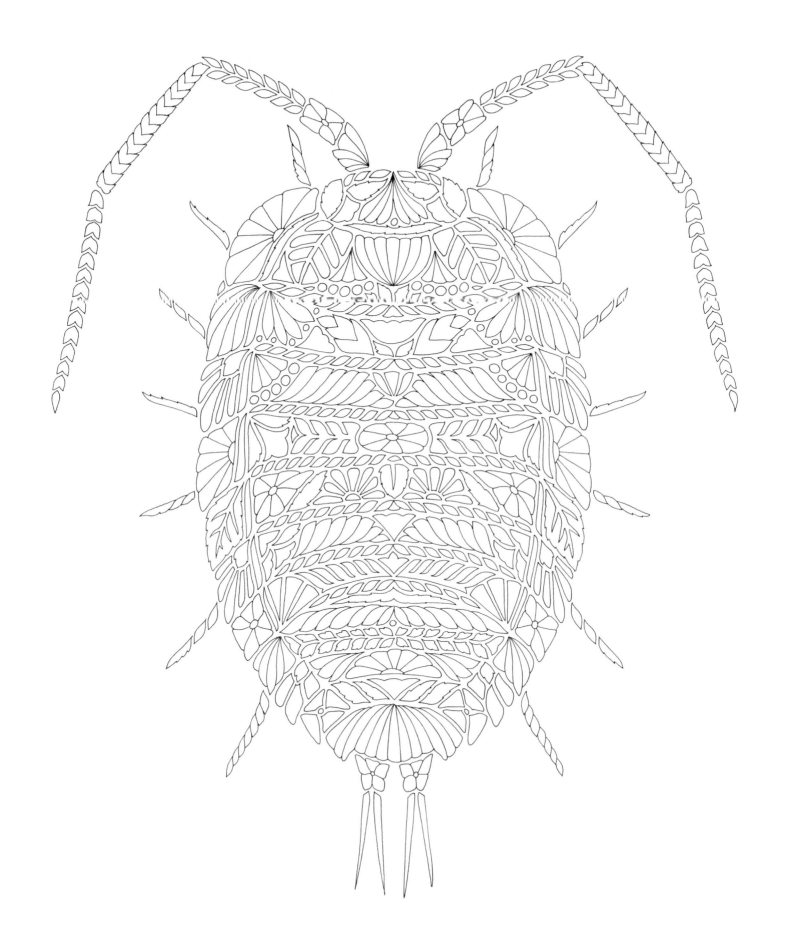

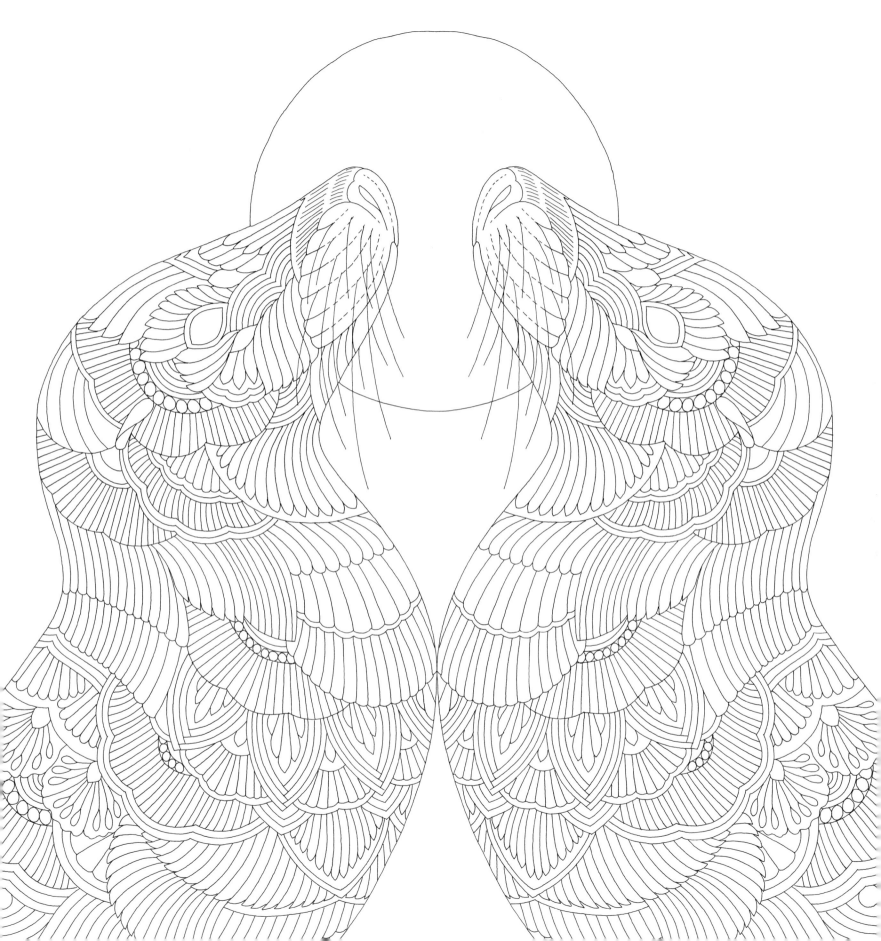

List of Creatures in *Secrets of the Sea*

In order of appearance:

Humpback whale
  (*Megaptera novaeangliae*)
Yellow-flanked fairy wrasse
  (*Cirrhilabrus ryukyuensis*)
Shell of a scallop (from family
  Pectinidae)
Hawksbill sea turtle
  (*Eretmochelys imbricata*)
Short-beaked common dolphin
  (*Delphinus delphis*)
Peruvian pelican (*Pelecanus
  thagus*)
Squat lobster (*Galathea squamifera*)
Soft corals (from order
  Alcyonacea)
European shag
  (*Phalacrocorax aristotelis*)
Starfish
  Royal (margined) starfish
    (*Astropecten articulatus*)
  Arctic cookie star
    (*Ceramaster arcticus*)
  Cake sea star (*Anthenea aspera*)
  Marble starfish / tile sea star
    (*Fromia monilis*)
Scalloped hammerhead shark
  (*Sphyrna lewini*)
Saltwater crocodiles
  (*Crocodylus porosus*)

Trumpetfish and pipefish
  Chinese trumpetfish
    (*Aulostomus chinensis*)
  West Atlantic trumpetfish
    (*Aulostomus maculatus*)
  Blue-striped pipefish
    (*Doryrhamphus excisus*)
  Black-breasted pipefish
    (*Corythoichthys nigripectus*)
Razorbill (*Alca torda*)
Atlantic puffin (*Fratercula arctica*)
Marine iguana (*Amblyrhynchus cristatus*),
  sea holly (*Eryngium maritimum*) and
  moon jellyfish (*Aurelia aurita*)
Japanese flying squid
  (*Todarodes pacificus*)
Garden eels
  Splendid garden eel
    (*Gorgasia preclara*)
  Spotted garden eel
    (*Heteroconger hassi*)
  Galápagos garden eel
    (*Heteroconger klausewitzi*)
  Giraffe spotted garden eel
    (*Heteroconger camelopardalis*)
  Zebra garden eel
    (*Heteroconger polyzona*)
Sea otters (*Enhydra lutris*)
Icon star (*Iconaster longimanus*)
Harlequin duck (*Histrionicus histrionicus*)
Arctic tern (*Sterna paradisaea*)

Blue button jellyfish (*Porpita porpita*)
Humboldt penguins
  (*Spheniscus humboldti*)
Common octopus (*Octopus vulgaris*)
Seabirds feathers
  Eurasian curlew (*Numenius arquata*)
  Arctic tern (*Sterna paradisaea*)
  Roseate spoonbill (*Platalea ajaja*)
  Greater flamingo
    (*Phoenicopterus roseus*)
  Ring-billed gull (*Larus delawarensis*)
  Common sandpiper
    (*Actitis hypoleucos*)
  Whiskered tern (*Chlidonias hybrida*)
Northern sea robin
  (*Prionotus carolinus*)
Little auk (*Alle alle*)
North American (West Indian)
  manatees (*Trichechus manatus*)
Reef manta ray (*Mobula alfredi*)
British Columbia wolf
  (*Canis lupus columbianus*)
Red-saddled anthias
  (*Pseudanthias flavoguttatus*)
Common cuttlefish
  (*Sepia officinalis*)
Inca tern (*Larosterna inca*)
Seaweed and algae
Polar bear (*Ursus maritimus*)
Puffadder shyshark
  (*Haploblepharus edwardsii*)

Jellyfish
  Purple-striped jellyfish
    (*Chrysaora colorata*)
  Spotted (lagoon) jellyfish
    (*Mastigias papua*)
  Fried egg jellyfish
    (*Phacellophora camtschatica*)
  Cannonball jellyfish
    (*Stomolophus meleagris*)
  Barrel jellyfish (*Rhizostoma pulmo*)
Vaquita (*Phocoena sinus*)
Grey seal (*Halichoerus grypus*)
Stingrays
  Yellow stingray (*Urobatis jamaicensis*)
  Blue-spotted ribbontail ray
    (*Taeniura lymma*)
  Spotted round ray (*Urobatis maculatus*)
  Round ribbontail ray (*Taeniura meyeni*)
Harlequin crab (*Lissocarcinus orbicularis*)
Various seashells
Sea snakes
  Yellow-bellied sea snake
    (*Hydrophis platurus*)
  Blue-lipped sea krait
    (*Laticauda laticaudata*)
  Spectacled sea snake (*Hydrophis kingii*)
  Elegant sea snake (*Hydrophis elegans*)
Ornate cowfish (*Aracana ornata*)
Sea slugs (*Chromodoris colemani,
  Chromodoris roboi, Hypselodoris bennetti,
  Hypselodoris maculosa*)
Majestic (blue-girdled) angelfish
  (*Pomacanthus navarchus*)
Coastal flowers
  Viper's bugloss (*Echium vulgare*)
  Shore bindweed (*Calystegia soldanella*)
  Sea campion (*Silene uniflora*)
  Sea aster (*Tripolium pannonicum*)

Walrus (*Odobenus rosmarus*)
Narwhal (*Monodon monoceros*)
Urchins (from class Echinoidea),
  seaweed and mermaid's purse (egg
  case) of the lesser-spotted dogfish
  (*Scyliorhinus canicula*)
Thorny (spiny) seahorse
  (*Hippocampus histrix*)
Ribbon eel (*Rhinomuraena quaesita*)
Butterflyfish
  Crown butterflyfish
    (*Chaetodon paucifasciatus*)
  Bluecheek butterflyfish
    (*Chaetodon semilarvatus*)
  Saddle butterflyfish
    (*Chaetodon ephippium*)
Emperor penguin (*Aptenodytes forsteri*)
Periwinkles
  Rough periwinkle (*Littorina saxatilis*)
  Flat periwinkle (*Littorina obtusata*)
  Common periwinkle
    (*Littorina littorea*)
Gulf signal blenny (*Emblemaria
  hypacanthus*) and blue-spot goby
  (*Pseudogobius olorum*)
Fiddler crabs
  Orange fiddler crab (*Uca vocans*)
  Blue (tetragonal) fiddler crab
    (*Uca tetragonon*)
  Watermelon fiddler crab
    (*Uca crassipes*)
  Thick-legged fiddler crab
    (*Paraleptuca crassipes*)
Anemones, urchins and coral
  Rock flower anemone
    (*Phymanthus crucifer*)
  Sputnik urchin
    (*Phyllacanthus imperialis*)

Watermelon zoanthid
  (*Zoanthus* sp. 'Watermelon')
Giant green anemone
  (*Anthopleura xanthogrammica*)
Sea slater (*Ligia oceanica*)
Short-tailed albatross
  (*Phoebastria albatrus*)
Sponges, coral and fish
  Sea goldie (*Pseudanthias squamipinnis*)
  Stove-pipe sponge (*Aplysina archeri*)
  Disc coral (*Turbinaria mesenterina*)
  Red coral (*Corallium rubrum*)
  Long sea whip (*Ellisella elongata*)
  Flowerpot coral
    (*Goniopora djiboutiensis*)
Orcas (*Orcinus orca*)
European eel (*Anguilla anguilla*)
Seahorses
  Pot-bellied seahorse
    (*Hippocampus abdominalis*)
  Slender (longsnout) seahorse
    (*Hippocampus reidi*)
  Tiger tail seahorse
    (*Hippocampus comes*)
  Lined (northern) seahorse
    (*Hippocampus erectus*)
Clown triggerfish
  (*Balistoides conspicillum*)
Galápagos sea lions
  (*Zalophus wollebaeki*)
Sea pen and feather star
  Phosphorescent sea pen
    (*Pennatula phosphorea*)
  Red feather star
    (*Himerometra robustipinna*)
Leafy seadragon (*Phycodurus eques*)

Test your colour palettes and materials here...

Also from Millie Marotta

Millie Marotta's Animal Kingdom: A colouring book adventure (2014)

Millie Marotta's Tropical Wonderland: A colouring book adventure (2015)

Millie Marotta's Curious Creatures: A colouring book adventure (2016)

Millie Marotta's Wild Savannah: A colouring book adventure (2016)

Millie Marotta's Beautiful Birds and Treetop Treasures: A colouring book adventure (2017)

Millie Marotta's Woodland Wild: A colouring book adventure (2020)

Millie Marotta's Island Escape: A colouring book adventure (2022)

Millie Marotta's Wildlife Wonders: Favourite illustrations from colouring adventures (2018)

Millie Marotta's Brilliant Beasts: Favourite illustrations from colouring adventures (2019)